THE PRIESTESS
AND
THE WHORE

COUNTDOWN TO WORMWOOD

PART ONE

BRITNEY EVERLONG

To Good Friends.

1

"So, when do we leave?"

Caitlyn Grove, sitting on the lap of her vampire girlfriend Claire Ashton, was trying desperately to win the argument they were having. Claire, having to suddenly leave Southtown with a mysterious, and not unattractive, stranger did not sit well with her. She felt that at least if she went along, she could be with Claire, help Claire. Unfortunately, Claire was not privy to Caitlyn's secret: Caitlyn's half-vampiric state. Caitlyn had sworn to her father many years prior that she would never reveal that to anyone, much less a vampire.

Claire raised her right eyebrow in protest. "*We* are not leaving. *I* am leaving, in about an hour."

"You have got to be kidding me!" Caitlyn protested. "I can't just stay here while you go off and face...*bad things!* Please, Claire, don't make me stay here!"

Claire shook her head. "No way in hell. Where we're going is just too fucking dangerous. It's a stronghold of the enemy, I'm not going to expose you to them. Forget it!"

Caitlyn, with a glower, slid off Claire's lap. "I swear to God I don't know who's worse; you or my dad! Everything's always 'I'm trying to protect you', and 'There are horrible things out there'! I'm a freakin' adult, Claire. Probably more so than you."

"That's not fucking fair, Caitlyn!"

"Neither is leaving me here!"

Claire stood from the chair, standing as tall as she can, and looked down at Caitlyn, who was a bit shorter. "There are things in that city that scare me, Caitlyn, and I *won't* deliver you right to them! If they knew about *us*, they'd *exploit* you. *Hurt* you. Maybe even *kill* you. Or...worse...*turn* you."

"Why would that be so bad? I want to be more like you!"

All of a sudden, Claire's eyes turned black as obsidian, but turned back just as quickly. Caitlyn started to back away from Claire slowly, as if terrified. Claire scowled at Caitlyn as she cowered, almost snarling. "No. You *don't*. There's not a day that goes by that I don't wish I *weren't* like this! And they would *twist* you, Caitlyn, and turn you into more of a monster than I am! I am *not* allowing that to happen. No. You stay *here*."

Caitlyn crossed her arms and looked away from Claire. "Fine. I think you *should* leave."

Claire walked out of Caitlyn's house and let the door slam behind her. Caitlyn fell to her knees after the door shut and cried harder than she had since Ben had disappeared. She'd promised herself she wouldn't let this happen again, but there she was, with a broken heart once more.

Caitlyn sat in her living room, despondent, surrounded by empty bottles of whiskey. She wasn't drunk, though; her body metabolized the alcohol almost as fast as she could consume it. It angered her more than anything that there was no escaping her foul mood, nor the remembrance of being left behind by the person she loved.

Her body ached, in part from mild alcohol poisoning, but mostly from wanting Claire near to her. It went through her mind over and over again; how could Claire just leave her behind? Wasn't she enough? Caitlyn knew she could take care of herself, but of course she couldn't tell Claire that. She sighed in resignation; these secrets were already fraying her relationship like a slowly snapping cable.

It had been some time since Caitlyn had become one of the vampire's lovers, and she knew she wasn't the only one that Claire was intimate with, but she'd always felt that there was something special between Claire and herself, a bond that Claire just didn't have with anyone else. Maybe that was wishful thinking on her part, though, and Claire's actions seemed to be proof of that. She could give herself a migraine just trying to analyze every facet of what was going on, and right now, that was one thing she just didn't need.

She thought back to the day she met Claire at Perky Café, when Claire was clearly looking for a meal. Caitlyn knew that she would prove irresistible to the vampire, but what she hadn't planned on was finding herself falling for the awkward and slightly crazy vampire. Even less expected was finding the vampire falling for her. Now, things felt so cold and distant between them, as if Claire, even though she insisted that leaving her in Southtown was for her safety, had other plans on her mind that most definitely didn't involve her.

She angrily tossed a bottle at a chair and roared with rage and pain. If Claire had just said she wanted to fool around with the new man she found, she would have been fine with it. Caitlyn understood that Claire wasn't a monogamous person, but why lie? Why hide it?

"Why do I keep falling for frickin' vampires?" Caitlyn yelled to no one. Her mind drifted back to her first relationship after Ben, and how Siobhán had betrayed her to, of all people,

Rex Mundy, a.k.a. Jesus himself. She couldn't help but find parallels, and her mind punished her because of them.

A knock at the door interrupted her flagellation. "Come in," she moaned. "I could use someone to tell me how stupid I am."

Becca Kauffman, one of Caitlyn's close friends, walked in the door. She'd taken to looking quite butch these days and had dropped a lot of weight. It was hard to tell her from a man of her age, and she was happy that way. She'd even started dating a lovely woman she met at one of the Gay Quarter's street festivals; in short, everything was looking up for Becca.

Becca saw the atrocious mess that Caitlyn had made, and just shook her head. "Bitch, you're straight edge for a reason."

Caitlyn started to uncontrollably sob. "Becca! Nothing fucks me up! This sucks!"

Becca cleared a few bottles away and sat down next to Caitlyn on the floor. "Yeah, I bet it does. Hey, I know you're all torn up over your girlfriend, but you can't just sit here and cry forever. Why don't we go get some coffee, huh?"

Caitlyn started to cry again. "That's where I met her."

Becca rolled her eyes. "We don't have to go to Perky. There's always Astro Java, there's Dunkin', there's a dozen places."

"I'd rather go to Perky."

"Caitlyn, don't make me hurt you."

Caitlyn and Becca walked over to Perky Café, the sun still high in the Indiana sky. The leaves were just starting to turn, and the September air was just starting to get that autumn crispness. As they walked down Peach Street, a few cars came and went, but the city of Southtown still had that sleepy northern Indiana feeling that always seemed to make you feel like things were safe, even though just underneath the veneer was a horrific rot of darkness and evil that remained incomprehensible.

A rot of which Caitlyn was a part.

Caitlyn's tears dried in the early autumn breeze as the two friends walked down Thurman Road towards Perky Café, and though she still spoke only of the one who'd broke her heart, she did so with far less hysterics. She knew that things would inevitably change in any relationship over time, and sometimes people grew apart, but she did not want to give up on Claire yet. She knew in her heart that she was in love, and when she was in love, she gave her all to the relationship; that was just how she was.

They finally arrived at Perky, and took a seat in the back, though not at the table where Claire and Caitlyn had met. Becca ordered two Molecular Hyperdrives and brought the steaming coffees back to the table. Caitlyn took a tentative sip, and, finding it wasn't too hot, took a much bigger sip. A weak smile crossed her face as she looked at Becca.

"Thanks, Becca. I think you're the best friend I have."

"I *know* I am," Becca replied. "I felt a disturbance in the Force and came to check on you. Now, what happened?"

"Claire went on some job out of town with some guy and she refused to take me with. Said it wasn't safe for me."

Becca raised an eyebrow in disbelief. "That's it?"

"What do you mean, 'That's it?' That's a horrible thing! We haven't been apart more than a few hours since we got together!"

Becca placed her fingertips on her temples. "Caitlyn, sometimes people go and do shit without you. It's part of being human."

"Claire isn't human."

"She's *mentally* human," Becca replied, exasperated. "It counts."

"But what if she cheats?"

"Then you deal with it *if* it happens. Life works like that. You deal with it as it comes. You can't spend your whole life worrying about things that haven't happened yet; you'll drive yourself insane."

Out of the corner of her eye, Caitlyn noticed a familiar sight; outside of the café, a person that shouldn't be there was walking by, a woman with pale skin, dreadlocks pulled back into pigtails, dark makeup, and leather clothing.

Mandy Blaze was walking past Perky Café. The woman who wrecked her life.

Caitlyn rose and dashed to the door of the café, throwing it open and rushing outside. When she got there, no one seemed to be on the street at all, not for several blocks. Had she imagined it? That was impossible; she had clearly seen Mandy there, but there was nowhere she could have disappeared to, no alleyway or side street for Mandy to turn down and disappear after the café. Caitlyn felt her hands ball up into fists, and her jaw clench. Something just wasn't right. Mandy had been there.

"Hello, Caitlyn," that damnable voice rang out from behind her. Caitlyn spun around slowly, and sure enough, Mandy stood there, just the same as she had been on the day she took Ben. "You look well."

"Bitch…" Caitlyn grumbled, her teeth grinding together with nearly-inhuman force. "How…dare…you…"

Mandy recoiled slightly. "Oh, my…I see you're still a little upset over…what was his name? Ah yes, Benjamin. He turned on you so quickly, you know. I was surprised how quickly he chose to be with me. But that is not why I'm here, Caitlyn."

Caitlyn was seething with rage and freshly-exposed pain. "Then get to the point," she snarled.

Mandy smiled. "I came to offer a deal. Would you like your dear Ben back?"

Caitlyn was struck silent for a moment. She knew that Ben had been changed into…something else, something that served a mysterious "Mother", but now Mandy was offering her his freedom, his return, but to what? To her? To normalcy?

She was with Claire now, and she could never go back to the way things were with Ben again.

"What's the price?" Caitlyn growled.

Mandy smiled, the kind of cold smile you see on crocodiles. "I need your help. Something only you can do. Vajra?"

From what seemed like thin air, a tall, slender Indian man stepped up to just behind Mandy's left side. He had dark glasses on and an expensive-looking suit. His expression was a serious, unflinching scowl.

Mandy turned to the man, and then back to Caitlyn. "This is Vajra. He…is one of the blood. He does some work for me, but a situation has come up that requires a more subtle approach, a perfect task for someone of your…unique…talents. If you complete the task Vajra needs completed, I will release Ben to you. Just as he would be without…enhancement."

Caitlyn paused to consider. She despised Mandy and everything about her, but to free Ben from her grasp, to relieve him of the existence he currently had to bear, perhaps it would be worth it to do what was asked, even though she hated Mandy enough to harm her, perhaps even kill her.

"Fine," Caitlyn snarled. "Deal."

Mandy grinned. "I knew you'd be wise enough to see the logic. Vajra will fill you in on the details. I've got to go now. I doubt we'll see each other again for a while."

"Good," Caitlyn growled in response.

Mandy nodded politely, and turned and walked off, disappearing down an alleyway across Humphreys Street. Vajra, however, looked Caitlyn over and scoffed quietly with disdain.

"I am not sure why Ms. Blaze thinks *you* can manage this," he quipped.

Caitlyn smirked, and then faster than he could react, she snatched the sunglasses from his face and crushed them into a ball of shattered glass and twisted metal, which she then dropped into his hand, all within less than a second. "Probably because of that," she said in retort.

Vajra blinked once but recovered his composure quickly. "I see. You are Uncursed. I can smell it on you." He turned towards a large sedan parked across the street from the café. "Come. We have matters that require prompt attention."

"Hold the phone, dude," Caitlyn interrupted. "Somebody's gotta lock up my house."

"It's been dealt with," Vajra replied. "Your father was contacted, though he was…less than ecstatic."

Caitlyn found herself giggling at the thought of a complete stranger contacting Ken Grove and letting him know that someone is borrowing his daughter for "reasons". It was likely they heard, at an unreasonable volume, every known profanity, and even some invented ones.

"Alright," Caitlyn said, "then I guess we're as good as we're gonna get."

Caitlyn had had her fill of vampires after Siobhán's betrayal. If she hadn't had such an immediate attraction to Claire, she would have just let the vampire go on her way that night in the café. She still didn't have much love for the vampires, even with her romance with Claire being what it was, for she knew well that for every Claire, there were a hundred Siobháns or Persephones. One of either of those nearly ended her life; any further would have to be thoroughly vetted before Caitlyn would ever again trust a vampire.

That being said, as the roads became less and less familiar, she found herself wondering just what it was that this Vajra needed from her, and why she was even considering helping the monstrous whore that destroyed her life and abducted and…changed…her boyfriend.

"Where are we going?" Caitlyn asked.

Vajra smirked. "Las Vegas," he replied.

Caitlyn remained silent for a moment.

"I'm sorry, what? I thought you said 'Las Vegas'."

"That's because I did," said Vajra, his smirk still very much in place. "I generally don't lie."

Caitlyn, now much more unsure of what was going on, found herself wondering if she was going to ever see Southtown again.

2

Vajra drove as fast as he could without attracting much attention, barreling down the highway towards Indianapolis. He sat silent and expressionless behind the wheel, making for a very uncomfortable trip for Caitlyn. His stern expression, unchanging as the stone, gazed only forward, as if she were not there at all.

"Still pissed about the sunglasses?" she asked, half joking.

There was no response whatsoever from Vajra.

"Guess so," said Caitlyn, shrugging.

A long silence fell over the vehicle as it careened towards the state capital.

"They were very nice sunglasses," Vajra mumbled, almost inaudibly.

"I'm sorry, I just couldn't think of any other way to show you what I could do without freaking out everyone in the café. You have to worry about that kind of thing, you know."

"You are telling me this? I am a vampire, child. I have lived for centuries by not 'freaking out' the populace."

Caitlyn mirthfully giggled at Vajra's overemphasis of "freaking out". Even though the vampire still wasn't smiling, she found herself grinning at the sheer absurdity of going on a road trip with a vampire she didn't know. She didn't trust him, of course, and would do her very best to fight him if she had to, but for now she was having fun with it.

"So…Vajra…I'm assuming you're Indian, right?" she asked.

"That is partly correct. I am Punjabi; there was no 'India' when I breathed."

"What does your name mean?"

"It means 'thunderbolt' in Hindi. It was given to me by my maker."

"Your…maker?" she asked, slightly confused.

"The one who turned me into what I have become, yes. Now if you don't mind, this is not a subject I care to discuss with mortals."

"Except I'm not *just* a mortal, am I?"

Vajra sighed. "No, I suppose not. But do not think I intend to give up any secrets to you."

Caitlyn giggled again. "No, I don't think you will. Maybe, though, you *could* tell me what I'm supposed to do in Las Vegas."

"That I *can* do. It is a simple matter. There is a vampire there who is an obstacle to my…employer. They need to be…dealt with, removed from the picture, even temporarily. When that is done, you will be well compensated for your efforts."

Caitlyn raised an eyebrow. "What makes you think I can stop a vampire?"

Vajra grinned, a grin of savage delight. "Word gets around quickly in certain circles. It is well known that you defeated the vampire Persephone."

"With help! Another vampire jumped her from behind!"

"And you will have help again. Do you really think I am just going to kick back and watch as you fight an ancient vampire?"

It was at that moment that the dire import of the situation finally hit Caitlyn, and it became clear just *why* Mandy wanted to send *her* on this task. It wasn't because

Mandy thought she *could* do it, it was because Mandy thought she *couldn't*.

Caitlyn silently swallowed as the realization washed over her like a tsunami. "Do…do I want to know *which* vampire this is?"

"Probably not," Vajra answered, in a very matter-of-fact tone. "But it is Yasmeen al-Shadaari herself we seek, though you probably know her better as Allison Finley."

Caitlyn's eyes widened in shock and horror as fear - true, genuine fear - slammed into her brain like a concussive blast. The name was more than familiar; it was the name of Claire's ex, who was the daughter of one of the oldest vampires in existence. It was this same vampire that had disposed of Persephone with relative ease, and Caitlyn had nearly been killed by Persephone.

Caitlyn swore under her breath as she realized that Mandy had never intended for her to return alive and had never intended to relinquish her grip on Ben. Mandy had intended for only one thing; she had intended for Caitlyn to die. Even with Vajra along to help, he no doubt was a lesser vampire of an uncertain lineage, one that could not manage Allison on his own, or they wouldn't even need her.

"Fucking Mandy…" Caitlyn muttered, *sotto voce*.

"I would be cautious about how you refer to Ms. Blaze, young one," Vajra quipped. "She has a terrible habit of hearing you when you think she can't."

"Who the hell even is she?" Caitlyn asked.

"You know," Vajra continued, "I asked her that myself once. Her answer was short and succinct. She merely said, 'The priestess and the whore'."

Caitlyn looked at Vajra in confusion. "'The priestess and the whore'? What does that even mean?"

"I'm afraid you'll have to ask her. I still don't understand it myself."

Frustrated and still with no answers besides believing that she was now marked for death by the woman that had already stolen so much from her, Caitlyn sunk uncomfortably into her seat, waiting to see what would come after they passed Indianapolis.

Night had fallen by the time they arrived in Indianapolis, and Vajra had felt it was a good time for them to stop. Caitlyn needed a break, and he needed a bite to eat, so they went their separate ways for a few minutes. Though she was sorely tempted to run off and hitch a ride back to

Southtown, some strange sense of needing to challenge herself, to push the limits of her powers, kept her there. She was leaning on the side of the sedan when Vajra returned, a grin on his normally-stern face.

"I take it you were…successful?" she asked.

"I rarely fail," he answered, the grin only widening.

They got back into the car and began to speed off, getting onto the highway towards St. Louis, and the next leg of their journey. For some reason, Vajra was humming a familiar tune, making Caitlyn do a double take.

"Why are you humming 'The Safety Dance'?" she asked, trying not to laugh.

Vajra himself laughed. "As my maker is fond of saying, not every vampire listens to harpsichord music. I personally enjoy the music of the Eighties."

Caitlyn's eyes widened with amusement. "I wouldn't have taken you for a Duran Duran guy."

"Are you joking? 'Rio'? 'The Reflex'? 'Hungry Like the Wolf' is practically the vampire anthem!"

Caitlyn could no longer contain the laughter and began to loudly giggle.

Vajra shot an evil glare her way. "Alright, smart girl, what do *you* listen to?"

Caitlyn caught her breath enough to speak. "Debussy, Dvorak, Liszt, Mozart mostly, but sometimes I put on…" Once again she began giggling.

Vajra seemed irritated. "Sometimes you put on *what*?"

"The Raging Pigfuckers."

Caitlyn had upgraded to full-on belly laughs now, and Vajra actually seemed to have joined her. "That's a real band?"

"Ish."

A moment of amused silence passed between them.

"What's it like, to feed from a person?" Caitlyn asked.

Vajra was stunned by the question. "Why would you ask such a thing?"

"I'm Uncursed…part vampire…I don't need to feed like you do, but I suppose I can, and my girlfriend is a vampire and feeds from me all the time…"

"Oh, I'm quite certain she does," Vajra interjected. "Your blood is like nectar and ambrosia to a vampire, and it just keeps regenerating. You have no idea how much self-control I'm needing just to leave you alone."

"So it's not because she loves me?"

"Oh, she may. But her feeding from you? You are a *delicacy*, young one. A rare commodity. In fact, the *only* known one alive."

Caitlyn pondered that for a moment. Did Claire actually love her, or was she just enamored of her delicious blood? Vajra, though he was a prick, was telling her a lot of information, intentionally or otherwise, that was making a lot of sense out of why Claire did the things she did, and very few of those things actually seemed to be out of actual love. The feeding, the showing up at all hours to fuck and feed, the overprotectiveness, and most of all, the ability to just run off with some random guy when the mood struck her.

Did Claire love her? It wasn't looking good.

"So what's it like? You didn't answer my question?"

Vajra scoffed. "How am I supposed to describe the feeling of someone's life draining down my throat? It's like for a brief moment we're one person, alive and whole, and I get to feel that life again for that moment, feel that warmth. It's intimate, as intimate as things can get."

Caitlyn breathed in deeply, her mind coming up with one of her classic bad ideas. "Pull over."

Vajra complied, not sure what was going on, and pulled off onto the shoulder of the road. Caitlyn stepped out of the car, and looking up and down the road, saw that there were no lights, no nearby homes, and no oncoming traffic. Vajra got out as well, with a confused look on his face.

"What the hell are we doing, kid?" he demanded.

Looking around with her enhanced senses, Caitlyn could see that there was nothing but some local wildlife nearby, and that nothing lurked in the pitch black to interfere. "Feed from me."

"Hold up, whoa," Vajra replied. "I just told you that might not be a good idea."

"I want you to do it. There's something I need to know."

Vajra stared at her for a tense moment. His expression of puzzlement changed into a look of inner turmoil as the part of him that was that craving, that primal hunger began to win out over his common sense. "For just a moment, and no more."

Vajra approached her slowly, his forehead wrinkled with worry and consternation. When he was close enough, he took Caitlyn by the shoulders and, lowering his head to her neck, bit in just enough to puncture her jugular vein, letting the natural venous flow pump the blood into his mouth. Once it hit his tongue, however, he found it one of the most delightful elixirs he'd ever sampled in both life and death, and he found himself wanting more, but he knew he could be carried away by the intoxicating, heady brew that was the blood of the Uncursed. He released her, and the wound closed of its own accord.

Vajra's head spun in one direction as the world around him spun in the other. Caitlyn, however, stepped back from the vampire, confused and somewhat frightened. After a moment, the almost narcotic effect of the blood seemed to have passed, and Vajra regained his composure.

Caitlyn, however, saw that the blood did not drive Vajra into a passionate frenzy; she could only assume that it was not in fact her blood that drove Claire to arousal, but something else. Perhaps her fears *were* unfounded after all, and Claire was still hers.

"Did you find what you needed?" Vajra asked.

"Yes," Caitlyn answered. "Let's get moving."

Morning had come, and Caitlyn rubbed her weary eyes, greeted by the Gateway Arch that let her know they'd arrived in St. Louis. Looking over at Vajra, she could see that he was squinting terribly, his eyes nearly closed. One thing Claire had taught her was that vampires did *not* actually burn in sunlight, but they *were* almost blinded by it, due to their enhanced senses. That made sense; Caitlyn also found herself needing sunglasses more often than not, even on overcast days. She felt terrible for crushing the vampire's sunglasses, especially now that he needed to see.

"Let's stop somewhere so I can get you some sunglasses, alright?" Caitlyn said. "Let me make up for, you know."

"Those were $400.00 sunglasses, child," Vajra snipped. "But yes, it would be lovely to see properly."

They managed to locate a shopping mall and took some time off of the road to allow Caitlyn a moment to stretch. Caitlyn, true to her word, first picked out a pair of sunglasses for Vajra that seemed to look similar to the ones she had crushed. Almost too similar, she noted with a wicked grin. Vajra, accepting the sunglasses with relish, placed them over his eyes, and almost sighed with relief.

"You have no idea how much better this feels," Vajra said, relief clearly permeating his voice. "Now I can think a whole lot clearer."

Caitlyn smiled, feeling like she'd done something to help someone, but a part of her mind reminded her that this was still a savage vampire that was likely taking her to her death. Her mind flashed back to the feeling of his teeth in her neck, and even though he released, there was always the chance that he might not have, a chance that she always took trusting Claire with her safety. For the first time since she fell in love, she found herself feeling doubts.

Would Claire always let go before utterly devouring her? Was she willing to bet her life on it?

Vajra seemed to regain his stern demeanor once the sunglasses were upon his face and gave Caitlyn a sober glance. "Whatever you need to do here, I'd do it quickly. I want to make Kansas City before nightfall."

Caitlyn nodded, and made her way into the bathroom, where she slumped down on the toilet. She needed a moment to herself, for the weight of everything that had come to pass had started to feel insurmountable to her. Between Mandy's reemergence, this suicide mission she was on, and being saddled with a vampire she didn't even know on this cross-country road trip, it was all just too much, and she needed silence. She quietly pounded the side of the stall with a balled-up fist, trying hard not to give in to the urge to cry.

Suddenly, a surge of hot pain hit her lower lip as she found herself awkwardly biting down, which surprised her. The pain felt like…

Caitlyn ran a finger under her front teeth and found something that shocked her: the points of her canines had somehow sharpened and extended by almost a quarter of an inch. She leapt off of the toilet seat and dashed for the closest mirror, and sure enough, the mirror revealed what her touch had told her; she had rudimentary fangs. She backed away from the mirror slowly in disbelief, not understanding what was going on. She was not a vampire, and had never been turned by one, and yet here she was, showing the characteristics of one. What was happening to her? Why now?

Once she left the bathroom, Vajra looked at her with a curious expression. "Did something happen in there?"

Caitlyn's face drained of all color, which was a feat in and of itself, as she tried to find words with which to respond to Vajra's question. "Um…I mean…"

Vajra cut her off with a raised hand. "I ask because you smell different than when you went inside. Your scent is…more like one of us."

Caitlyn was unsure of how to reply to that. She had no idea what was going on with her body, but her mind was still mostly clear, albeit wracked with worry and anxiety. She was uncertain of what the correct reply was; if she told him the truth, he might take exception and kill her, whereas if she lied he might discover the truth and kill her. It seemed a bit of a no-win scenario, so she chose to do what her father had always told her to do in these situations.

"Something is happening to me. It's like my vampiric characteristics are becoming stronger."

She chose the truth.

Vajra's forehead deeply furrowed faster than she could see it happen, and his usual scowl grew more wrathful. "Open your mouth."

Caitlyn sighed and acquiesced; upon opening her mouth the vestigial fangs she had somehow sprouted were there, and Vajra seemed concerned and confused at the same time. "Shiva's dance…I understand now why Persephone feared you so much."

"Feared me? She tried to *eat* me."

"This is truth, but for a reason. She knows what you are, what you represent. You are the next step in the evolution of both human and vampire, and it terrifies the eldest of our kind because you possess all of our strengths…"

"And none of your weaknesses?"

Vajra smirked and let loose a chuckle. "You have your own weaknesses, of course, and Persephone knows them well. You can be assured that others of our kind know them just as well."

"So, they're going to hunt me down," Caitlyn grumbled.

"Very likely."

Caitlyn's head hung just slightly as the reality of her situation hit her. What Vajra said was true; the more vampires knew about her, the more they'd hunt her. Already she had Persephone on her tail, so how long would it be until she had a whole slew of ancient vampires chasing her down, craving her blood?

"However," Vajra interjected, "there is one advantage you possess. According to the legends, you can use blood arts, assuming that you can find someone to teach you."

"I don't suppose you're willing to teach me?"

"I am not. Besides, if the old stories of the Uncursed are true, you…will have to feed first."

"Feed? As in…"

Vajra nodded, with a sadistic grin. "As in, like we do, drink the lifeblood of mortals."

Her stomach turned at the thought of biting into someone's flesh and drinking the very blood from their veins. Her life was already soaked with blood; she did not relish the idea of having to consume that blood just to have abilities beyond what she already possessed. She already had superhuman abilities that were nothing to take for granted. She was stronger, faster, more agile than anyone alive she could think of, so what more could she need?

Vajra raised a finger to his lips and grinned. "I take that back. I *will* teach you some basic blood arts, if…*IF*…when we get to Kansas City, you hunt and feed from someone I choose. You do that, I will teach you some useful tricks that you will need when you get to Vegas."

Caitlyn blanched at the thought of Vajra's challenge, but maybe, just maybe, it could give her an advantage over whatever enemies were coming, and a chance to protect those she loves from those same enemies.

It might even help her get Ben back.

"You're on."

Revolting as the idea of biting someone was, sometimes you just have to make a sacrifice for the betterment of all, and in this case, Caitlyn was fairly convinced this was the way.

Vajra's crocodile smile, however, was not so convincing.

3

It was just past sunset when the car passed into Kansas City, and Caitlyn found herself dreading the oncoming night. Vajra had all but dared her to feed as a vampire does, straight from the source, and to say she had reservations was quite the understatement. The vampire wore a cruel smile on his face from the moment the sun hit the horizon, drinking in Caitlyn's uncertainty and trepidation as if it were the very sanguine humor itself. Every time she would shift uncomfortably, he would smile even wider, until his amusement could not be contained any further, and he had to act on it.

He pulled the car over in a quiet neighborhood and shut off the motor. Removing his sunglasses, he seemed all the more intimidating with his dark eyes now wide with sadistic glee. "You are now going to enter this house," he said, gesturing to the home in front of which they'd parked, "and you are going to feed from the person, or persons, who live there. If you successfully do so, I will teach you some tricks of the trade, so to speak. Fail to do so, and I will mock you relentlessly all the way to Las Vegas. Understood?"

Caitlyn nodded, though in no way did she want to do any such thing. She thought about what her father would

[37]

think, or her mother, or even Claire, who sought to shield her from the majority of vampire goings-on. What would Becca say about her indulging the monster within her? She couldn't help but think they would all be mortified if they saw what she was about to do, but if there was a chance that she could get an edge on Allison Finley…

Would it be worth someone's life?

"Do I have to…kill them?" Caitlyn asked, her stomach doing nervous backflips.

"Do I have to kill them?" Vajra said, mocking her. "Of course, you'll have to kill them! Do you want assault charges brought against you? You don't have any powers that erase memories, I assume?"

Caitlyn shook her head slowly, her face turning beet red with embarrassment.

"My point is made," Vajra continued. "We live in a secret world, Caitlyn. A world that must stay secret, regardless of how 'uncursed' you might be. When you feed, you have two options: erase their memory or end them. There is no other option. Now go, do what you must."

"Allyn? We're going to be late for the concert!"

Skye Garrett had been looking forward to this concert for weeks, and nothing was going to stand in her way, not even her fiancé. Her favorite musician, the goth-rocker Miasma, was coming to Kansas City for one night only, and she'd managed to score two tickets.

"These things take time, love," Allyn Thomas yelled back. "My eyeliner has to be on point."

Allyn and Skye had met two years prior at a local goth club, and it was dark love at first sight. Skye was fond of introducing Allyn as the one person who wore more makeup than she did, which was true most of the time, but they were inseparable as a couple. Allyn had proposed to Skye a month prior at a Cyanotic show and had even presented his fiancée with a black diamond, which she accepted with her typical zeal. Most people found them to be fascinating people, the least morbid goths alive, but they both had a zest for life that few could match.

Skye burst into the bathroom, nearly ramming into Allyn, who was hunched over and staring into the mirror, fine-tuning his eyeliner. "C'mon! I need to finish up too!"

Allyn rolled his eyes. "No one told da Vinci to hurry up."

"Yes they did!" Skye screeched. "All the time!"

Skye planted her face right on Allyn's neck and left a huge, black kiss mark there atop his carotid artery. He gasped in horror and reached for a makeup wipe. "Bitch!"

"Hoe!" Skye replied, as she redid her lipstick.

The two lovers were laughing and enjoying their makeup application upstairs, while downstairs, the front door quietly opened. Caitlyn peeked her head inside, and not seeing anyone nearby, silently stepped into the house. She deftly shut the door behind her, as quietly as she'd opened it, and then listened carefully to any sounds in the house. She could hear two voices coming from the second floor: a man and a woman, both young, probably in their twenties. One person would have been simple; two was much harder.

As quietly as she could, even for someone with preternatural reflexes, Caitlyn crept through the house. She wasn't familiar with the layout of the place, so she had to guess as to which room was what. The voices had come from the upstairs, so she made her way to the stairwell, hoping for no loose boards that would creak and give her away. The last thing she needed was a criminal charge, or worse, getting shot at by some crazed homeowner. The stairs were solid, and more importantly, quiet, so she crept upstairs towards the voices.

Caitlyn inhaled deeply through her nose once she reached the top of the stairs. She'd only recently taught herself to be able to know the distinct scents of individual people and wasn't proficient enough to know who each scent belonged to, but she could discern one scent from another. There were only two in the house, and no others that she could tell. No dog, no animals of any kind that she could tell, just a man and a woman. She could see the light coming from a room down a small hallway, and shadows moving in that light. Both people must be in that room, she surmised, but it would be tactically advantageous to separate them. How to do that, though, was a whole different matter.

Without warning, she could hear footsteps coming from the room, and a woman stepped out. She reminded Caitlyn a lot of Claire, though this woman was as thin as a pencil. She was also heavily made up wearing shiny leather and latex. Metal hung from her neck and face, and Caitlyn was certain that it was hanging from several other, unseen, spots as well. She wore platform thigh-high boots adorned with chains and metal skulls. The woman walked across the hall into another room and shut the door behind her.

Caitlyn made her move, suddenly emboldened by a scent she hadn't noticed before. It was like a meaty, and yet metallic scent, something that made her mouth water, coming from that room with the light. She crept slowly and silently along the wall in the hallway, one eye on the door the woman had disappeared through, the scent of metallic meat growing stronger with every step, becoming almost maddening as she approached.

Once she reached the doorway of the room with the light, Caitlyn peered inside, seeing a well-apportioned bathroom, and a man in full Victorian-goth regalia working on his carefully-done makeup in the mirror. Caitlyn slid into the room, hoping his attention was focused completely on his mirror, slowly creeping up on the man with his perfect hair, his perfect makeup, and his fancy goth style. She managed to slide behind him and rose slowly, waiting for the perfect moment.

Allyn was satisfied with his makeup and looked into the mirror one final time to admire his handiwork, but there was something wrong; there was Caitlyn, pale-skinned, with long, straight, red hair, standing behind him, and she looked hungry.

Her reflexes took over, and she leapt at him, immobilizing his left arm with hers, and though she was hesitant, she knew now what the scent was, and why it was driving her crazy; it was the scent of blood, and the part of her that was vampire was craving it. She clamped her mouth down on his jugular vein and her small fangs managed to do the job, piercing his blood vessel and starting the flow of the hot, tangy lifeblood into her mouth.

She didn't find it repulsive as she thought she might; in fact, it was quite enjoyable to her, and that troubled the human part of her, but that part was not in control at the moment. The vampire was in full command at that moment, and it drank deeply. Allyn's eyes closed in ecstatic bliss, and Caitlyn took some delight in knowing that her kiss also gave pleasure, just as Claire's did. Allyn fell to his knees, and Caitlyn let go, licking the wounds and watching them slowly close.

Allyn turned to her, his eyes wide with fear and lust. "Holy shit! I mean…you're real!"

"I…um…I mean, yeah, but…"

At that moment, Skye came darting around the corner, barreling into the bathroom. "Allyn, we gotta…" Upon seeing him on the ground, and Caitlyn standing over him, she let out a piercing scream that threatened to shatter windows.

Allyn scurried to his feet, trying to placate his frantic fiancée. "No, no, Skye, it's okay! She…she's a…she's a vampire!"

Skye stopped screaming and turned to look at Caitlyn, her head slightly cocked. "Really?"

Caitlyn, not sure how to respond, simply nodded.

Skye's eyes widened and she smiled almost as wide as her eyes. "That…that's so cool! I mean, I saw the stuff on the news, with the video, but I just thought it was a fake. And then here you are." She helped Allyn to his feet. "Did she bite you?"

"Yeah," Allyn replied. "It was pretty intense."

"Okay then," Skye said, baring her neck to Caitlyn. "Do me!"

Caitlyn inhaled again, trying to catch the woman's scent. Sure enough, the scent of blood was there, but there was something else, something *off*, about her blood. It turned her stomach, and she shook her head. "I…I'm sorry, I can't."

Skye's expression turned from wonder to one of shock. "You know, don't you?"

"Know what?" Caitlyn asked.

Skye looked to Allyn, who nodded to her, and then back to Caitlyn. "I have HIV. I've had it for years. It's under control, and as long as we're careful, I can't get Allyn sick, but it's there. Somehow you know, don't you?"

Caitlyn hung her head, feeling genuinely bad for the other woman. "I…didn't know exactly what, just that there was something wrong. I'm…new to this."

"It's cool," Skye said, a look of astonishment on her face. "I can't believe it. There's a real vampire in our house. This is so badass!"

"And the bite didn't even hurt very long," Allyn added. "It hurt at first, but then…it was almost…"

"Enjoyable?" Caitlyn asked, sarcasm heavy in her voice.

"Well, yeah, actually," Allyn continued. "I felt almost…connected to you, in some weird way, and it was an intense, pleasurable sensation. It was a rush."

Caitlyn gritted her teeth, trying not to bite through her tongue. He wasn't wrong about how the bite felt, and it angered her, because it meant that it was the same for her, and it was just one more way that it looked like the vampire in her was becoming stronger. In the moment, she had enjoyed giving the man pleasure rather than pain, but now if she read between the lines, it meant that there was a terrible metamorphosis going on that was not by her choice.

She whispered a silent prayer that she wasn't becoming a full vampire, though she had a full belly of stolen blood that suggested that her supplication may have come too late.

"I have to go," Caitlyn said as she turned to leave.

"Please…" Allyn interjected as he slid into her path. "Please, let us go with you."

"Allyn?" Skye questioned, unsure of what the man was doing.

"Don't you get it, Skye?" Allyn fired back at Skye. "This is it. This is the big thing we've been looking for! Forget all the concerts and the goth clubs; all that stuff never brought us any real fulfillment."

Skye looked at Allyn with incredulity. "Well, no, but…"

"This is a *real* vampire!" Allyn continued. "Just think about what we could learn from her!"

Caitlyn sighed with absolute regret; of all the houses in all of Kansas City, she had to pick the one with people that would venerate her as some kind of deity. She also thought of Vajra, and what he'd say to having to fully mortal acolytes in tow, rather than just flat out killing them. Then again, she reasoned that it would be better than leaving them alive and able to talk about what they'd experienced…

"Fine," Caitlyn finally said, after a moment of silence. "But you're paying for your share of gas. And your own food."

Allyn and Skye both agreed, and threw some clothes in a bag, following Caitlyn out to the waiting car. Once they all climbed in, Vajra lifted his sunglasses, looking at the two new caravanners, and then looking at Caitlyn in disbelief.

"What in the undying fuck is this?" Vajra demanded.

"Would you believe, it's a long story?" Caitlyn replied, shrugging her shoulders.

"A story I suggest you start telling me immediately," Vajra snarled, anger beginning to be evident in his tone.

"Well, you said I should hunt, and I did. I drank from him, which went fine, until I was interrupted by her, and she was screaming, and he stopped her, and they just sorta…followed me."

"Why did you not kill them?"

"I couldn't feed from her. She has…blood issues. And him, well, he tastes good."

Vajra remained silent for what felt like hours, his strong jaw clenched hard. When he finally spoke, it was with great tension and incredible irritation. "They are your responsibility. You clean up their messes."

Vajra turned back to the steering wheel and started the car. He remained completely silent the entire time they traveled back to Interstate 70, and his seething presence kept everyone else silence as well, though Allyn seemed to want to ask a question. He leaned over to Skye, trying to whisper in her ear.

"Do you think he's…"

Caitlyn snapped around quickly, glaring at them with almost as much annoyance as Vajra. "Yes, he is. A very, very old one, so do *NOT* piss him off, please and thank you."

There was not a single word spoken by anyone the entire time the four of them were in the state of Kansas.

Sometime after they had crossed the border into Colorado, Vajra stopped off at a rest stop along the interstate so the mortals could do mortal things and he could find some dinner as well. Skye and Caitlyn departed into the restroom, and Allyn walked into the AxisBurger shop, famished as ever. Caitlyn stopped in front of one of the slightly filthy sinks with its spotty mirror and took a moment to splash some water on her face. Skye walked up to her, a look of concern on her face.

"Are…are you okay?"

"Is it that obvious?" Caitlyn replied. "Not really."

"Hey, umm, it's okay about Allyn," Skye continued. "I'm not jealous or anything."

Caitlyn weakly chuckled. "It's not that. I would have done the same to you if not for…well, you know…"

"Then what?"

"Can you keep a secret?"

"Sure," Skye replied, not entirely a lie.

"I'm…I'm not really a vampire. Not completely. I'm half vampire."

"What? How's that even work?"

"You know, I'm still trying to figure it out too," Caitlyn chuckled once again. "I didn't even know I had fangs until yesterday."

"Wow. That is wild," Skye said. "I mean, what a mind fuck, right?"

"Tell me about it," Caitlyn said. "My dad knew about it before I did, and he didn't want me to know I had any of these abilities in the hopes that I wouldn't use them."

"Jesus. That's kinda like how my ex didn't tell me he had HIV until after we had sex."

"He *what*?" said Caitlyn. "Now *THAT'S* fucked up."

"Yeah. Son of a bitch *claims* he didn't know. He's full of shit."

Caitlyn sighed. "Guess we both got fucked in the deal. We have something in common after all."

Skye extended her hand to Caitlyn. "Skye Garrett."

Caitlyn smiled weakly and accepted the handshake. "Caitlyn Grove."

Skye smiled as well. "Now we're not strangers, and I don't have to call you 'ma'am'."

With a heartfelt giggle, Caitlyn imagined anyone calling her "ma'am". She'd always been younger, smaller, slighter than most people, even with her enhanced abilities. In truth, if one didn't know Caitlyn, they'd be inclined to think her a bit mousy, even nerdy, depending on how she dressed. Caitlyn, however, used her appearance as a weapon, cultivating an image that led to others underestimating her; she'd done this since grade school, and it was a never-ending source of irritation for her father. With Skye and Allyn, however, it was a different story, because they knew of her unusual heritage before they even knew her name, and worse still, they came back for more!

Then again, was it so different from her relationship with Claire?

She knew who and what Claire was from the second she walked into Perky, and yet she still chose to go home with her and get very intimate with her. She fell in love with Claire even though she knew Claire was a vampire. On the other hand, Claire had no idea that Caitlyn was anything but a very athletic but otherwise very normal woman.

Perhaps Caitlyn found this adulation from Skye and Allyn to be so odd because there were no secrets; she knew what Skye hid and both Skye and Allyn knew what Caitlyn hid. Everything was out on the table, and that scared Caitlyn a little.

It scared Caitlyn even more when she realized that she was holding Skye's hand. She didn't know when it had happened, nor did she know why. She panicked when she realized what was going on and yanked her hand away from Skye, and both of them stood in that restroom, awkwardly looking at each other.

"Why did you do that?" Caitlyn asked.

"I didn't," Skye replied. "*You* took *my* hand."

A moment passed in silence, with the two women looking at one another. Caitlyn turned and walked out of the restroom without saying a word, though thoughts flew through her mind with alarming rapidity.

4

Caitlyn sat in the front seat of Vajra's car, completely silent, the world rushing by as she stared out the windshield, unmoving. Internally, however, all was chaos; she could not keep her thoughts from going back to that awkward moment between her and Skye.

What even was that moment? It was something Caitlyn could not even begin to understand. She had not felt any sort of attraction to the woman when she had met her; if anything, she was put off by the scent of the virus that dwelt within Skye, even if it was in such a minute quantity that it was functionally harmless. Caitlyn would know it was there. She would *always* know it was there.

There was no conversation in the car. Indeed, the only sounds that could be heard were the sounds of the engine, the tires on the road, and Allyn devouring his Triple Axis with cheese. Caitlyn turned slightly to see what Skye was up to, only to see the woman asleep, leaned against the outer wall of the car. She sighed with relief, for if Skye was asleep, she probably didn't think much of the brief exchange. It couldn't mean much, after all, because Caitlyn was already with someone, and regardless of Claire's predilections (though Caitlyn held out hope that Claire would be faithful), *she* wouldn't be the one to cheat.

Her mind calmed somewhat at seeing Skye asleep as well, for the very idea of temptation was discarded. It was simply two people indulging in a gesture of honest friendship; it had to be. There was no attraction there, no sexual temptation whatsoever.

Yet Caitlyn found herself looking at Skye again and again. Skye was beautiful, to be sure. Her skin, a rich mocha color, contrasted beautifully with her body jewelry and her bright pink hair. She wondered just where else Skye hid piercings, but dismissed such thinking quickly, worried about where such thoughts would take her.

She also found herself looking at Allyn. He was quite attractive as well, now that she wasn't trying to eat him. He was fit, athletic in a way similar to the way she was, though the billowy shirts did him no favors, the skin-tight leather pants did, but Caitlyn drove those thoughts from her mind as well. She couldn't entertain the notion of any sort of desire for anyone but Claire.

And yet…

By the time they reached Denver, night had fallen, and the immortal contingent of the caravanners had decided to stop for the night to allow the fully mortal contingent time to rest. Vajra went off to hunt alone, and that left Caitlyn on her own to wander the streets of the mile-high city, alone with her thoughts. It was for the best at that time for her to be alone, for thoughts of forbidden fruit grew harder to resist the more she tried to fight them. She, who had helped put a stop to the machinations of a vampire so ancient and powerful she'd been worshipped as a goddess, was defenseless in the face of her own libido.

Caitlyn found a quiet spot, on the side of a mountain, overlooking part of the city, where she could sit alone and think. She was fairly certain no one would find her here. She sat down on a grassy patch and rested her head on her knees, near tears.

"Caitlyn?"

The voice, coming from behind her, startled her almost to the point leaping to her feet. Her head whipped around, only to find a very contrite Skye standing behind her.

"I'm…I'm sorry, I followed you," Skye continued. "I…need to talk to you."

Caitlyn sighed and gestured to the grassy patch next to her.

"Well…where to begin, right?" said Skye. "I know things got…awkward…before, but I was glad about it. When you came into my life, everything changed. I didn't know there were such things as vampires and monsters and magic in the world, but then you showed up and opened the door to a whole new world…and I'm grateful…but there's more…"

"Skye, please…" Caitlyn interjected.

"I need to say this," Skye said, cutting her off. "Please. I felt something when we touched hands. I think…I think I'm falling for you."

Caitlyn's stomach sank into the earth beneath her. How could this be true? She'd only just met this woman, this woman who was with the man who's likely still in the car. The very thing Caitlyn was afraid to hear, she'd heard. What's worse, part of her was glad to hear it. Part of her, however small, desired her too…

"Skye…I…I'm…"

"You're with someone, I know. I know. But for just tonight, can you just…"

Skye carefully brushed a stray lock of hair out of Caitlyn's face, their eyes locked. Caitlyn was trembling, as was Skye.

"…can you just be with me?"

Their faces, their lips, were so close together now, and Caitlyn's resolve was spent.

"Yes."

Their lips met in a passionate kiss, as their hands took hold of each other. Skye gently laid Caitlyn down on the cool ground and mounted her, writhing hungrily as they continued to kiss and caress each other. Caitlyn threw aside all resistance and gave herself fully into the moment, for there was no point in stopping now; the deed was done.

Some distance away from the two women, a silent observer watches from the shadows of the nearby forest. He is unmoving, save for the clenching of his jaw at what he sees, his teeth grinding in ever-growing rage.

"Why do you make me do this?" the observer asked, in a low, gravelly voice.

"Because you must see," a female voice responded from behind him. "You must see so that you understand."

"I'm tired of your riddles, witch," the observer snarled.

The woman laughed and leaned in close to the observer's ear, whispering to him. "I'm no witch. I am the priestess, and I am the whore, but I am no witch. When I have finished my priestly duties, I can be your whore…but only then."

She bit his earlobe and ran her tongue down his neck as she disappeared into the dark of the woods. The observer, enraged, unfurled huge wings and vanished into the night sky.

Caitlyn lay on the ground next to Skye, their arms intertwined. All they had done was kiss and grope each other, and they hadn't even taken any clothes off, but somehow she felt closer to Skye than she'd ever felt with Claire. There were so many problems that their tryst caused, though, but she dismissed them for the moment; all she wanted was to feel Skye's heart beat next to her.

Was she in love? The emotions she was experiencing now were very different from what she felt with Claire. What she felt in Claire's arms was raw, primal, intense. Claire made her want to get naked and fuck to exhaustion. Skye evoked different emotions in her; a deep, painful hunger in her heart had been sated in Skye's arms. Skye somehow made Caitlyn want to just stay there forever, on this grassy patch outside of Denver, in the arms of this incredible woman who had so many struggles and yet still stood tall and proud.

Skye made her want to be better than she was. Claire just made her horny.

"Caity?" Skye said, breaking the silence.

Caitlyn winced slightly; no one ever called her that but her father. "Mm?"

"If we're gonna work, there's gotta be some things we have to figure out."

Caitlyn giggled. "Yeah. A lot of things."

"I'm being serious."

"So am I." Caitlyn started to worry. Admittedly, anxiety was one of her oldest foes; any psychologist worth a damn could publish for years on just her alone.

"I'm not leaving Allyn."

Once more, Caitlyn's stomach sank into the cold earth. After all that, after she let her defenses down, she set herself up for a shot right to the gut.

"However, if you're open to it, and he's open to it, I'm not opposed to we three becoming 'we'."

Caitlyn looked confused for a moment. She'd heard of polyamory, of course, but in Southtown, Indiana, you just didn't get that sort of thing. Still, Allyn was a decent enough person, and definitely attractive, but could she do that? Could she share herself with two people? Could *she* share Skye with another person?

She smiled, her eyes sparkling in the dim glint of the street lights as she looked in Skye's beautiful brown eyes. "I guess we better have a talk with Allyn."

The sound of Allyn's snore could be heard from several feet away from the car as he peacefully slumbered. He would not hear how it was drowned out for several seconds by the buzzing of insects.

Caitlyn and Skye slowly walked back towards where the car was parked, hand in hand, happily smiling. Suddenly, they heard a horrible shriek coming from that direction, and Caitlyn looked at Skye, who nodded.

"Go," Skye said.

Caitlyn sprinted at her full speed back to where the car was parked to find a scene out of nightmare; holding a thrashing, struggling Allyn by the neck was, somehow, Persephone herself, wickedly grinning, fangs bared.

"Hello, bitch," Persephone spat.

"Oh, fuck me," Caitlyn muttered under her breath. "How the *hell* are you even here?"

Persephone smirked. "I'll just keep that to myself, thanks. Now, you're going to surrender yourself to me."

"And if I don't?"

"I uncork this little wine bottle."

Caitlyn cursed under her breath. She knew what the cost was, but she had an advantage that Persephone couldn't know about. Hopefully didn't know about, at any rate.

"Okay. Okay. Let him go, and I'll go with you."

"No tricks, Caitlyn. I know your capabilities." Persephone narrowed her eyes.

Caitlyn raised her hands in front of her, palms out, in a sign of surrender. Persephone slowly let Allyn down, and he coughed violently as he tried to draw breath. Caitlyn then walked alongside of Persephone, trying to figure out the next step.

At that moment, Skye came around the corner, and saw what was going on, and shouted at the assembled folk. "Hey Caitlyn, is Allyn alright?"

Skye's shout distracted Persephone for only a fraction of a second, but it was enough for Caitlyn to move. She leapt backwards and landed on Persephone's back, tightly grabbing on to the thrashing vampire. Baring her own fangs, Caitlyn drove them into Persephone's neck as hard as she could. Instead of latching on and drinking, she focused more and tearing and shredding flesh, trying to do as much damage to Persephone's blood vessels as possible. In her frenzy, Persephone tried desperately to throw Caitlyn off, but instead managed to lose almost all the blood she had. After several long, tortuous minutes, the ancient vampire finally fell to the ground, drained and inert. Caitlyn spat a final chunk of artery out at the withering corpse.

With Persephone out of the way, Caitlyn turned her attention to Allyn, who seemed a little roughed up, but otherwise fine. Skye was tending to him as Caitlyn approached.

"That," Allyn remarked, "was badass."

"I'm sorry about that, Allyn. It shouldn't have happened. It's my fault."

Allyn smiled at Caitlyn. He had a nice smile, warm and honest. "It's fine, really. We came with you looking for some adventure. God knows we found some, right baby?"

Skye and Caitlyn looked at each other, and both giggled. Allyn grinned. "My answer is yes, by the way."

"What?" asked Skye, sounding genuinely confused.

"You were going to ask me if we could bring Caitlyn into our family. I say yes."

Caitlyn's jaw dropped open in astonishment. "How did you…"

"You think I didn't notice how you were so chatty going in to the bathroom but utterly silent leaving it?" said Allyn, a broad smile on his face. "I know when someone's got it for someone, and you two have it for each other just like Skye and I have it for each other. I'm pretty sure in time you and I will get closer as well, so it sounds good to me."

Caitlyn smiled with delight, and Skye laid a light kiss upon her lips, and kissed Allyn as well. "This is so exciting!"

"So where are we going to live?" asked Allyn.

"The bottom of a deep hole if you don't go to sleep and be quiet, humans," growled Vajra, suddenly appearing from the shadows. "Tomorrow is all the way to Vegas, so be prepared for the long haul. We're starting early, so…what in the hell is that?" He looked at the bled-out corpse by the car, his spidery finger extended and quaking angrily.

"We…had a run-in with one of the local vampires," Caitlyn lied. "Not a big deal."

Vajra snarled with irritation. "Fine. Hide it in the brush and then go to sleep. It's a long day tomorrow. Even longer night, especially for you."

Just before sunrise, the car shook to life as the five occupants loaded in, this time with all three breathing caravanners piling in the back seat in a mass of cuddling, kissing and otherwise annoying Vajra with their mortal affection. Vajra could not help but roll his eyes at the jovial mood of the mortals and their keeper as they frolicked and teased one another. He knew that very soon the party would end, and he would be the harbinger of its demise. Still, it was fortunate that he had a guaranteed way to motivate the uncursed girl; she would do anything to keep them from harm, regardless of the risk or the cost. She was foolish in the extreme, and that was exploitable in a situation of need. Yasmeen el-Shadaar was no easy target, but with the uncursed as bait, a very clever trap could be set, one that even the infamous daughter of the Light Keeper herself could not escape.

Vajra had played this game for a very long time, and the key to any trap was irresistible bait. The uncursed was as irresistible as it got.

As Vajra schemed, the new threesome enjoyed each other's company in the back seat. Caitlyn felt very comfortable in between Allyn and Skye; indeed, she felt safer there than she could remember feeling for a very long time. Though everything had happened so fast, she did not doubt the veracity of the affection she received and that she returned. It felt every bit as real as she'd felt for Ben, and in some ways even more real than she'd felt for Claire.

Claire was now a problem, a problem that she would have to solve, and solve quickly. Eventually, she would have to tell Claire that it was over, but how exactly do you break up with a vampire? What if she took it poorly and went on a rampage? Then again, it would be a lot worse if she found out on her own. No, Caitlyn knew she had to tell Claire, because she was very much in love with Skye; she knew that now with all her heart. The attraction between Skye and herself was irresistible, and there was definitely a spark there between Allyn and herself as well, even if it wasn't as hot as with Skye.

It was the right thing to do, but she was terrified about doing it. There were so many unknowns about dealing with a jilted vampire, especially one as young and volatile as Claire.

She was almost tempted to ask Vajra if he would work security for the breakup.

Vajra. The great enigma. Caitlyn couldn't trust him because he was so guarded about letting anything about himself slip into conversation. People with nothing to hide throw information about themselves into chatter all the time; most people love to talk about themselves. Vajra never talked about himself except once, when he said he was Punjabi, and that was only because he was insulted at being called "Indian". She'd ridden across most of the country with him and knew next to nothing about him beyond him being a Punjabi vampire.

Suddenly, a beeping sound shook everyone out of their respective reveries, and Vajra reached inside his jacket and pulled out his phone. "Yes?"

A voice could be heard, but it was impossible to hear what was being said, but Vajra seemed extremely displeased. "You're the boss. Alright. At the Nevada border. Yes. Bye."

Vajra noticeably sped up after disconnecting the call and seemed extremely irritated. "Caitlyn, Miss Blaze wishes to meet with you once we get into Nevada."

Caitlyn's smile vanished. Somehow, Mandy Blaze was going to worm her vile way back into her life once more, and she feared for what might come of it. However, since Mandy was the backer of this whole excursion, Caitlyn supposed she might as well meet with her, if only to tell her to fuck off.

"Who's 'Miss Blaze'?" Skye asked.

"A real bitch," Caitlyn explained. "She stole my first boyfriend and…well, let's just say she's made my life very painful."

"Then why would she want to see you?" asked Allyn.

Caitlyn sighed. "I don't know. Maybe to rub it in more?"

"She's not stealing *this* one," Allyn growled.

"She better not," Skye responded, slapping him lightly on the back of the head.

Caitlyn giggled nervously, but the specter of Mandy Blaze was now hovering over her head like Damocles' sword, and with Mandy, the thread was ready to break at any moment. She had a feeling of unavoidable dread, as if something terrible was about to come over the horizon, something that would change her life forever.

5

Vajra slowed the car down just over the border into Nevada, pulling in to the first gas station he could find.

Caitlyn looked around as they came to a stop, parked in a space next to a woman on a motorcycle. She wore a helmet with a reflective visor, so she could not see the woman's face, but somehow Caitlyn knew who it was. The shiver down her spine told Caitlyn everything she needed to know.

"Out," Vajra commanded, and Caitlyn did as she was bidden.

Once Caitlyn exited the car, the woman got off of the motorcycle and removed her helmet. The woman had long, straight, black hair, but her face was very much that of Mandy. Mandy seemed to have eschewed her normal gothic look for no makeup, an old bomber jacket and jeans. Something seemed *off* somehow, as if Mandy wasn't the same as she normally was.

"Caitlyn," Mandy said, in her lilting tone that Caitlyn despised.

"What do you want?" asked Caitlyn, her tone curt and abrupt.

Mandy smiled, that predatory smile she shared with reptiles. "Walk with me. I want a soda."

Caitlyn scowled, but followed along anyway, wanting to know what Mandy's endgame was going to be. Mandy sauntered slowly towards the convenience store attached to the gas station, drawing all eyes as she went, reveling in the attention, and driving Caitlyn to fury. Mandy opened the glass door to the store and the cashier audibly gasped when he saw her. All Caitlyn could do was roll her eyes.

"Come, the soda is over here," Mandy said, motioning for Caitlyn to follow.

Caitlyn's fingernails dug into her palms almost enough to make them bleed, but she followed, nonetheless. Mandy opened one of the cooler doors, unzipped the bomber jacket a little to reveal no shirt beneath, and fanned herself with the cool air.

"The desert is so very hot," Mandy said, "and I've been riding a long time."

"Get to the point," Caitlyn growled.

"In due time, Caitlyn dear," Mandy said, her smile widening. "Would you like a drink?"

"I would like to get the fuck away from you."

Mandy turned and looked Caitlyn dead in the eyes, her smile vanishing for a moment. "That is not going to happen." Her smile returned, as if it had never left. "It's so very hot in the desert, please, let me get you a drink."

"Fine, whatever. Psycho Cola."

Mandy nodded. "A fine choice. I believe I will have one as well." She grabbed two bottles from the cooler and took them up to the cashier, who couldn't seem to remove his eyes from her breasts. Once they were paid for, she handed a bottle to Caitlyn. "I think perhaps a more…solitary location would be best for our talk, don't you?"

As Mandy finished her sentence, Caitlyn looked around to find herself in the middle of the deep desert, with no structures, vehicles, or people around in any direction. The oppressive heat seemed to close in upon her like a vise, and she took a small sip from her soda. "How did you…"

"Do you understand what it is that I do, Caitlyn?" Mandy asked.

Caitlyn's fists balled up tightly, painfully, until her knuckles were white. Her rage was starting to boil over, and all she wanted was to just finally take a swing at the woman who had taken everything from her. "What do you mean?"

Mandy laughed. "It's a fundamental question, dear one. What do I do?" She took a sip of her soda and closed her eyes for a moment. "I give people what they want. Our dear Ben wanted a dangerous fuck, and I gave him that. Vajra wanted someone to give him guidance after you went and wrecked poor Persephone, and I gave him that. And you…" Mandy took another sip, her blood-red eyes looking right at Caitlyn. "You wanted someone to hate, someone to blame for everything that has happened to you, and voila! You have a nemesis worthy of someone of your level of power."

Caitlyn felt her fangs drop into her mouth. "You know nothing about what I want."

Mandy laughed again, this time the mockery not held back. "My dear, I know everything about what you want. Do you really see yourself so enigmatic? So arcane? You blame me for the loss of everything that held you back, kept you just a mere human, but you are so much more, aren't you? You should be thanking me for removing the obstacles that kept you from your evolution."

"I just want my life back!" Caitlyn screamed.

Mandy smiled and took another sip of her soda. "No, you don't. You just want the trappings of that life to make you feel in control. But there is a better way, Caitlyn. Join me."

Caitlyn stopped dead in her tracks. "Excuse me?"

"Join me, Caitlyn, and I can show you the true extent of what you can do. You're neither mortal nor vampire, but something else entirely, something that neither has ever seen, and both fear."

Caitlyn scoffed. "I'd sooner give myself to Persephone."

"You may have to, dear one."

Vajra started the car and popped the locks open, turning around to face Allyn and Skye.

"Out."

He did not need to say it a second time. Allyn and Skye dashed out of the car quickly and Vajra drove off with alarming speed.

"No, I stopped her. I beat her. Bled her out in Denver." Caitlyn uncomfortably shifted her stance.

Mandy smiled and took another sip of soda. "It's cute how you still think that was the real Persephone."

"What do you mean?"

"You really are slow on the uptake, aren't you, my love?" Mandy said, laughing. "Illusions can affect more than just one victim. In this case, an unfortunate vampire suddenly believed she was an ancient, just as you did."

"How did…"

Mandy silenced her with a wave of her hand. "Enough questions. It's time for me to talk."

Caitlyn found herself completely immobilized by some immense force, and though she struggled with all her strength, she could not move more than an inch or two at most.

"Do you know who I am yet, Caitlyn? Have you ever had even the faintest clue?"

"Besides being a shitty neighbor and the bitch that stole my boyfriend?"

Mandy smirked at Caitlyn's indictment. "These are true, but I am so much more than that."

"I don't care who you are, I just want to be rid of you."

Mandy turned towards Caitlyn, outstretched her hand, somehow pulling Caitlyn towards her. "Many have tried, but I'm not so easily dismissed. You see, what you see here, this body, is but a mere shadow."

"Let me guess; you're Cthulhu, aren't you?"

Mandy laughed again, this time downing the entire soda. "An amusing story, but not quite." The invisible iron grip around Caitlyn seemed to fade, letting her fall to the ground. "I am that which dwells in the horrible dark between universes. I have a thousand eyes in a thousand universes. My reach extends beyond anything you are capable of understanding, my love."

"Bullshit. You're just a person. A *crazy* person."

Mandy laughed once more. "It was my hand that created you from the blood of the Wordless and the seed of Man. You are meant to be my vanguard. You know I'm right, Caitlyn. Think about your dreams…you already know my name."

Caitlyn froze with fright; since she was a child, she had chilling dreams about being trapped in a dark place with *something*, something terrible that spoke a single word to her. There was no way Mandy could ever know about the dreams, for she had never spoken of them to anyone, her father included. Even now, the word she'd heard spoken in that terrible voice haunted her. Mandy was right, she knew the name, but she feared to speak it, for fear of someone hearing it, for fear of opening a door that could never again be closed.

Mandy no longer smiled. "Say it, Caitlyn. Say my name."

Caitlyn was frozen in terror and had no desire to speak anything. She only wanted to flee from this place, to get as far away from Mandy as she could, but she knew now that Mandy would follow her wherever she would run. There would never be any escape.

"Say it!"

Tears streamed down Caitlyn's face as she fought through panic, trying to figure out what to do. There was nothing else she could do, though. She had to comply.

"L'vz'ratha," she spoke, in a hoarse whisper.

Mandy raised her arms to the sky in jubilation. "Yes! Yes! You've finally figured it out! And now you know why you mustn't fight it, Caitlyn. We're meant to be a team, you and I."

"No," Caitlyn replied.

"There are countless worlds out there just meant to be ours, Caitlyn. Just embrace me and we will conquer them together.

"No!" Caitlyn shrieked.

Caitlyn leapt from where she stood, swinging as hard as she could at Mandy's jaw, and connecting with a bone-crunching thud. Mandy was knocked backwards several yards and slid on the ground several more after landing. Mandy lay still for several seconds, but finally started to slowly climb to her feet. Her face was horribly disfigured, her lower jaw shattered by Caitlyn's blow.

"Now really, wash that nesheshary?" Mandy said, clearly irritated.

Mandy's face seemed to fill back in at inhuman speed, but once it had healed, Caitlyn was on her again, this time striking her in the torso, crushing her rib cage. Each time Mandy would be knocked back several yards, and each time Mandy would rise again and heal completely, further enraging Caitlyn.

"Enough," Mandy finally said, raising her hand towards Caitlyn, immobilizing her again. "I can see you're not going to learn your lesson this way, so let's try something different." She looked at her watch. "She should be showing up just about now."

In the distance, a black Aston Martin DBX started approaching the place where the two women stood. When it finally arrived, a familiar blonde woman got out, looking very confused.

"What in the hell…" Allison Finley looked around, not seeing Las Vegas anywhere.

Mandy smiled. "Hello, Allison. I believe you're familiar with Caitlyn here."

"Uh, yeah. I was, heh, actually looking for her," Allison said.

"I would like to make a deal with you," Mandy continued. "Seems that Caitlyn here was contracted to take you out."

"By you!" Caitlyn screamed.

"Irrelevant," Mandy interrupted. "What we're going to do is have ourselves a little…contest. Allison, you win, you take Caitlyn prisoner. Caitlyn, you win, you go on your way, and we never meet again."

"Fine," Allison said.

"Let's go," Caitlyn muttered.

Out of the corner of her eye, Caitlyn could see that her father and another woman she didn't know were in the backseat of Allison's Aston Martin. She knew at that moment that there was a lot more at stake than just being rid of Mandy; her father's life was now at stake as well.

Allison made the first move, moving faster than Caitlyn's eye could see, and hitting Caitlyn square in the chest, knocking her back several yards and also driving the air out of her lungs. Caitlyn was left on the ground gasping for air, but not beaten. She called upon whatever reserves she had to move as fast as she could, and within a second she was within striking distance, and delivered a wicked uppercut to Allison's jaw, taking the vampire off guard and knocking her down.

"Impressive, for a mortal," Allison said, wiping a trickle of blood from the corner of her mouth. "But you're not an ordinary mortal, are you?" Allison bared her fangs and roared, the feral sound seeming to resonate with Caitlyn, because she responded in kind. "No, you're no ordinary human at all."

"I'm full of surprises, bitch," Caitlyn hissed.

"I'm nothing *but* surprises, child," Allison responded.

Caitlyn leapt once again, this time going for Allison's throat, but when she arrived, the vampire was gone. She lost her balance and landed awkwardly, falling on her face. She could hear the vampire laughing from some distance away.

"It's foolish to try, Uncursed," Allison mocked. "You can't beat me. You couldn't even beat Persephone without help, and she's far younger than I."

Caitlyn picked herself up off the ground. She could feel that one of her ribs was cracked and her head was spinning, but she refused to quit. "So what? Older doesn't mean better."

"It does when you're a predator."

The searing pain from her chest was starting to become too much, but Caitlyn could not, would not, surrender. "I won't let you win."

"I've already won," Allison laughed. "I have your father, and soon, I will have your dearest love. Claire will feast upon your very blood, and she will be free of mortal ties. She will be the monster I intended her to be."

"Fuck you!" Caitlyn leapt once more at Allison but was easily brushed aside with a blow that shattered her shoulder and collarbone. Caitlyn fell to the ground, screaming and writhing in agony.

"Delightful!" Mandy said, clapping her hands in glee. "We have a winner!"

Allison scooped up the shattered mess that was Caitlyn. She could hear Ken screaming in fear from the car, but Caitlyn was unable to do anything but bleed; she was beaten. Allison threw her into the front seat of the Aston Martin and fastened the seat belt, slamming the door shut behind her.

Turning to look at Mandy, Allison snarled at the giggling woman. "How do I get to Vegas from here?"

Mandy smiled. "Just go back the way you came. You'll find it soon."

Allison got into the car and sped off, and Mandy stood there, in the middle of the high desert, and smiled.

"It's finally begun."

6

Stranded at the gas station after being left there by Vajra, Allyn and Skye were left in a difficult situation. Everything that they had, all the belongings that they had brought with them, including their IDs, credit cards, and such were gone with Vajra. All they had was about fifty dollars in emergency cash that Skye always kept with her, and that wasn't going to get them very far. More than that, though, they were both intensely worried about Caitlyn; it had been almost an hour since Caitlyn had vanished along with the strange woman that clearly Caitlyn did not like, and they were concerned as to her whereabouts.

Allyn was busy trying to secure transportation to Las Vegas, though they did not know where to look, they knew Caitlyn would eventually be there. Skye, on the other hand, was trying to find the means to get hold of someone, anyone, that they knew and could help them out. Pay phones, sadly, had mostly vanished, and the ones that remained were all card-based. She eventually had to take the hit and buy a phone card, which allowed her to use one of the convenience phones at the station.

Allyn watched as a convertible pulled into the station, an expensive model, and he smiled when he saw its occupants; one was a tall man in all black leather with blue hair peeking out from under an odd black cap, and the other was an attractive, pale-skinned woman with long, black hair in jeans and an old One-Eyed Doll t-shirt. He slowly approached the car, trying not to seem like he was trying to carjack them.

The tall man looked up, adjusting his dark glasses. "Can I help you?" he said, in a thick German accent.

"Yeah, hello," Allyn nervously spoke, something about these two people setting him on edge. "My partner and I got stranded here and we were wondering if someone going into Vegas could maybe…"

The woman, wearing a cheap cowboy hat, turned and smiled at Allyn. "You need a ride into town, right?" She turned back to the tall man, batting her eyes. "Baby, can we help them out?"

The tall man, looking slightly annoyed, nodded. "If they are ready to go by the time we are done fueling, *Mädchen*. I would suggest that they hurry."

"He's a grump today, but it's all good," the woman said. "Go get your partner quick, and we'll take you into town."

Allyn shot them a friendly smile. "Thank you so much!" With that, he turned and ran off to find Skye, who wasn't far.

Skye hadn't had much luck getting any of her friends on the phone, so when she saw Allyn running up to her with a smile on his face, she hung up and met him half way. "We finally have some luck?"

"Yeah, decent couple are willing to take us into town, but we gotta go now!"

"Well then, let's fuckin' go!"

Skye and Allyn dashed back to the convertible and hopped in the tight squeeze of a backseat, not minding the closeness at all. The woman in the front passenger seat turned and extended her hand to the two new passengers.

"Hey. I'm Claire. Groucho over here is Erik. Buckle up, because my babe loves to drive fast."

With that, Erik gunned it, and the car sped off into the setting sun.

Allison found herself back on the interstate fairly quickly and chose not to think too much about it. Her dealings with Mandy Blaze tended to always have strange happenings surrounding them, but almost always ended in profit. The wrecked body of Caitlyn Grove was already starting to heal even now, before her eyes, but nowhere near as fast as a true vampire. It would not be a concern before they got to Vegas.

"You've never been anything but a menace, Allison!" Ken Grove screamed from the back seat. "Leave my daughter out of this!"

Allison smirked and quietly laughed. "And *you've* never been anything but a glorified juice box, so I would mind my tongue were I you." She turned back to Caitlyn in the front seat, who even now was looking more like a human than a wrecked pile of assorted meat. "All of you have one thing in common, you know. You're all obstacles to Claire becoming the vampire that she needs to become. For some unknowable reason, she still values each of you, but that's alright. By the end of the night, you'll all be little more than *hors d'oeuvres* for me and for Claire, and she will finally be where she belongs – at my side."

"Claire will never side with you over us, you fanged bitch!" cried Poppy Armitage, the woman in the back seat with Caitlyn's father. "She hates you!"

"No," Allison said, her annoyance increasing. "No, no, no, no!"

"It's true, Allison," Ken said, joining in with Poppy. "She hates you for what you did to her and when she finds out that you've done this, she will never forgive you."

"You're wrong," Allison hissed. "She still loves me, and she will love this gift."

Caitlyn's arm suddenly thrust upward and grabbed hold of Allison's throat, violently snapping her neck with a sickening crunch. Allison let go of the steering wheel, and Caitlyn grabbed it and yanked it to the side, guiding the car to the shoulder of the road. Once the car rolled to a stop, Caitlyn hopped out as quickly as she could, freeing the others with all speed.

"We gotta move," Caitlyn said, sounding very tired. "She won't be down long, and we can't be anywhere near her when she gets back up."

Caitlyn snapped the zip ties that held Poppy and Ken, and they all ran off from the Aston Martin as quickly as they could, nervously navigating the crumbling rocks and sand that began just off of the road. Once they got onto relatively solid ground, they could get some decent speed, but by that time, they could hear an unearthly shriek coming from the direction of the road, and they knew that there was no time left.

Moving almost too fast for eyes to follow, Allison came whistling towards them, murder in her eyes, but Caitlyn was able to get everyone out of the way before anyone could get hit. Caitlyn started to run off towards the deeper desert, and Allison followed her, her fangs bared for the kill.

"Keep moving!" Ken said, gesturing to Poppy. "We double back to the road, boost the car, and Caitlyn will meet up with us as soon as she can."

"I give a shit as long as it keeps that psycho away from us!" Poppy said, ready to leave.

As Ken and Poppy were trying to sneak back to the car, Caitlyn led Allison further out into the desert. Allison followed, with only blood on her mind, screaming like a banshee. Caitlyn suddenly shifted her weight, and Allison was unable to stop in time, and Caitlyn drove the point of her elbow directly into Allison's skull, splitting the skin and spraying blood all around. Allison's chin hit the ground from the force of the blow, and she skidded to a halt after a few yards.

Caitlyn wasted no time; she immediately leapt onto Allison's back and sank her fangs into Allison's neck, trying to take as much blood from her as she could. Vajra hadn't made good on his promise to teach her the vampiric blood arts, but she knew she was stronger after feeding, and if mortal blood made her strong, it only made sense that the blood of an elder vampire would be all the more potent. Allison thrashed wildly, trying desperately to get Caitlyn off of her, but the Uncursed held fast, drinking more and more of the precious blood within the older vampire.

Finally, Allison wrenched her right arm out of its socket and grabbed hold of Caitlyn with a grip like molten iron; her touch burned like fire and was utterly unbreakable. Caitlyn screamed in agony as Allison's left arm followed suit with a terrible crunch, and then using both arms, Allison slammed Caitlyn into the ground repeatedly, until a small crater formed. Caitlyn lay inside the crater, unmoving, and Allison's arms returned to their normal positions with hideous cracking sounds. Allison knelt down beside the unmoving body and whispered into Caitlyn's ear.

"I'm going to let Claire kill one of you," Allison whispered, "and then I'm going to kill the rest."

"So, Claire, where are you from?" Skye asked, trying to be amicable.

"Indiana," Claire answered, making a face as if she'd tasted something bad. "But I'm thinking of relocating to a better place. Maybe Vegas. I don't know. Baby, what do you think?"

"We could have stayed in New Orleans, *Mädchen*, had you not had such a…dispute with the local governor." Erik answered, sarcasm as heavy as his German accent.

"You always see the bad shit, asshole," Claire snapped. "Don't listen to this motherfucker. He's just being sour like he always is when we're on business."

"It is difficult doing business when you keep enraging our business partners, *Mädchen*," Erik fired back.

"Fuck my death," Claire said. "I can't with you."

"You love me."

"Yeah, sadly I do," Claire turned back to Skye. "How about you two? What's your story?"

Skye nervously chuckled, because something still felt a little *off* about their car mates. "From Kansas City. We were coming out to Vegas with a friend, but the son of a bitch stranded us in the middle of nowhere."

Claire frowned at that. "That's shitty. That's *real* shitty."

"We figure, we get to Vegas, we can catch a bus home with what money we have left, or maybe get ahold of one of our friends, and they can front us airfare, or something."

Claire nodded, and a half-smile crossed her pale face. "Well, Vegas isn't far, so hopefully you'll have better luck there than you have." She turned and grinned at Erik. "It's the right city for luck, right baby?"

"*Ja, Mädchen*, that it is," Erik said, now smiling.

A familiar KMFDM song started playing on the radio, and Claire started swaying in her seat. "This song is my jam! Turn it up, baby!"

Erik obliged, and for a moment, all four occupants of the car were forgetting their respective troubles and enjoying the heavy beat of the music. Claire was thrashing and swaying in the front seat, and Erik was singing along. Skye and Allyn both lip synced every word, and it was as if for a moment, there was no difference between the occupants of the car; they were all just fans of the band and enjoying a moment of loud bliss.

"Fuck!" shouted Claire. "I wish this moment would never end!"

Erik smirked. "A former co-worker of mine was fond of saying, *Mädchen*, be careful what you wish for, because you might get it."

In the distance, finally, the lights of Las Vegas could be seen, and everyone in the car was heartened. Skye and Allyn both breathed a little easier knowing that they would soon be on their own again, and hopefully find a way to be reunited with their partner. Erik and Claire, on the other hand, had other plans in mind, plans that had nothing to do with Skye and Allyn.

"There it is!" Claire happily said. "Whoo! Almost there!"

"Yeah," Skye said. "Can't wait."

Claire looked at Erik and pointed her head briefly at the two in the backseat. Erik shrugged, and Claire smiled again, turning back to face Skye and Allyn.

"Hey," Claire said, "you all like weed?"

"Uh, yeah, sure," Allyn replied.

"Fuckin' badass!" Claire said, excited. She dug around in a leather jacket that must have been hers, and pulled out a cigar and a lighter, handing them to Allyn. "Might as well blaze up before you get into town. Not much going on in Vegas besides booze, booze, booze."

Allyn lit the cigar and inhaled deeply, and as advertised, the core of the cigar was pure cannabis. He held the smoke in as long as he could, and then exhaled, the sensations almost immediately hitting him. He sighed in relief and pleasure, and passed the cigar to Skye, who repeated the process. Everyone passed the cigar around, deeply inhaling the fragrant smoke. After a few rounds, though, it was clear that Skye and Allyn were stoned out of their mind, and they both nodded off.

"Pull over, babe," Claire said, her tone changing to a far more serious one. "It's our turn."

Caitlyn regained consciousness sometime later, to find her hands and feet bound with handcuffs and zip ties. She struggled against them, but they would not budge. Nothing she did seemed to allow her any further freedom of movement, so she chose to conserve energy instead, giving up on struggling for the time being. She raised her head slightly and saw the lights of Las Vegas not far from where they were. She knew that whatever fate awaited them would be found there, and any chance she had at making it out alive would have to wait until they were there. She was bound and in a moving vehicle, and there were also other people, people who could not defend themselves in a fight against a lesser vampire, much less Allison Finley, who had to be protected. No, she had to wait until Vegas for any action.

"Good," Allison spoke, her voice raspy, as if her larynx was damaged. "You're awake. I need you intact and conscious when Claire kills one of you. I want you to experience the horror of the death, or the pain of your own death. I want you to suffer, you miserable Uncursed bitch!"

Caitlyn was still woozy, light headed from the beating she had taken, but her mind was clear enough to know that it wouldn't go well for her if she baited the vampire just now, so she chose to remain silent. It still seemed to anger the vampire regardless.

"Don't think I don't know about the 'relationship' you have with Claire, you vile aberration. You are a thing that should never have existed in the first place and should be cleansed. Something I will see to personally. She could never love an unclean thing such as you."

Caitlyn bit her tongue hard, trying not to speak, not to respond to the insults being thrown at her by the mentally unstable vampire. The urge to reply with a cutting remark was hard to resist.

"Do you really think she is in love with you? Even now, when she is on the road with another vampire? I would bet she has already given herself to him a hundred times over by now."

Caitlyn couldn't hold back any more. "If she did, she did." Fury was rising up within her, but she fought it down for the moment; now was not the time. "We will deal with it one way or the other."

"Big words, child, but that's all they are," Allison said, mocking her. "Big words from a little girl. Words that will fall silent once Claire silences them once and for all."

"I don't believe Claire could ever hurt me," Caitlyn said, with more hope than conviction.

"Then you are an idiot," Allison said, "not just a child."

Claire gently stroked Skye's cheek as the woman slept. There was something about her, something in the back of her mind, in the most animalistic part of her, that said there was something off about the woman, but Claire was determined to taste of her regardless. Allyn slept quietly next to her, and Erik was already feeding from him. Claire gently sank her fangs into the soft flesh of Skye's neck, and the sweet flow of cannabis-laden blood streamed into her mouth, and the warm sensation started to fill Claire's body just as the world started to echo and leave streaks of light in her vision.

Claire kissed the wound closed and slumped down in the front seat of the car. "Mother fuck, that is some good shit!"

Erik smiled and nodded. "I do not waste my time with anything but the best."

"Sweet Satan, I wanna fuck you right now," Claire said, as she was already removing her t-shirt.

Allison pulled her car into the parking lot at the Dungeon Hotel and Casino, right on the main strip. She pulled up alongside a tractor trailer and parked there. Seeing that there was no one in the truck, she took each of her prisoners and loaded them into the back of the trailer, making sure that they were secure, and most importantly, unable to escape.

"Now, Miss Grove, you're going to do something for me," Allison growled, pulling out her phone.

Claire, after feeding from Skye, was feeling quite stoned, and after a quick, albeit vigorous, session of bloody lovemaking with Erik, decided that she wanted to drive for a while. Erik, unable to deny her, slid over into the passenger seat as Claire hopped off of his lap and retrieved her clothes, which lay in a crumpled heap on the driver's seat. Skye and Allyn had not yet stirred, but the vampires were quite certain that they would soon wake, so it was imperative that they get back on the road quickly and get to Las Vegas with all speed.

"Alright, time to roll!" Claire shouted in jubilation. "Ahead warp six, Mister Data. Engage!"

Claire slammed on the gas, and the car shot forward hard enough to rouse the two sleeping mortals in the back seat. Slowly, Skye and Allyn began to wake, shaking off the effects of the potent cannabis strain that Claire had provided.

"What the fuck was that?" Allyn said, starting to sound angry. "Was that laced?"

"Nope," Claire said, keeping her eyes on the road. "One hundred percent Chemdog. Thirty-two percent THC to give you a lovely evening."

"Jesus," Skye responded. "No wonder it knocked us out. That's the premium stuff." Skye turned to Allyn, nudging him with her elbow. "You only ever get the weak shit."

"We *do* have bills to pay, you know," Allyn fired back.

It wasn't long, at the rate of speed Claire was driving, that they finally arrived in Las Vegas, past the iconic sign that welcomed them to the famed city.

"Where you wanna go?" Claire asked. "I can drop you anywhere."

"Airport would be best," Skye replied. "We can probably catch a bus from there, and I know I can find a phone."

Claire nodded, and they headed for McCarran International Airport, which wasn't far from where they were. Traffic was heavy, as this was the peak hour for the Vegas night life, but Claire managed to navigate it well, ably dodging both traffic and any police she saw. Finally, after several minutes of Claire's daredevil driving, and everyone else fearing for their lives, they pulled in to the airport parking lot, and both Skye and Allyn climbed out of the convertible.

Claire reached into her pocket and pulled out a thick roll of cash. She counted out fifteen one-hundred-dollar bills and handed those to Allyn. "That ought to help you get home on the next flight, alright?"

Skye and Allyn were astonished. "Uh, thank you!" Skye said. "You've been too kind to us."

Erik turned to them and smiled, a smile that somehow felt *wrong* to the pair from Kansas City, which seemed a little too reptilian. "Think nothing of it. We've all been there once or twice. Besides, we've enjoyed your company. It is the least we can do."

"Well, thank you again," Allyn said. "Hopefully whatever business you have goes well."

"Oh, I'm sure we'll make a killing, won't we baby?" Claire laughed.

Allison dialed Claire's number, banking on her infamous laziness and love of inertia. "Now the endgame begins for one of you." She laughed, a laugh devoid of humanity and tinged with madness.

The phone rang, and after a ring or two, a familiar voice answered. "Hello?"

Allison shoved the phone into Caitlyn's face. "Talk to her."

Caitlyn, tears running down her face, tried to think of what to say, and only a few words came out. "Claire…help me."

Allison then returned the phone to her own mouth and hissed angrily into it. "I have the people you love. They are going to die. You have a choice to make. Meet me outside in ten minutes." She then disconnected the call, turning her attention to the mortals with her in the trailer. "You will all die. You are FOOD!"

She leapt out of the trailer, shutting and locking the door behind her. Once she was gone, Caitlyn once again struggled against her bonds, and again to no avail. Suddenly, she remembered something she'd been told some years prior, and shifted herself to face away from her father.

"Dad!" Caitlyn whispered. "Do you have your platinum knife?"

"Yes, I do!" Ken said, remembering. "It's in my pocket, but you might be able to reach it."

Caitlyn scooted herself over right next to her father, close enough to reach into his pocket, trying to reach the all-important implement. Her hands finally fell upon it; the wooden handle of Ken's platinum plated pocket knife. She pulled it out slowly, trying not to drop it. She managed to drop it into Ken's waiting hand, and he cautiously opened it.

"Now cut my zip ties," Caitlyn said. "I can bust the handcuffs by themselves."

Ken, fumbling a little, managed to slice through the zip tie that bound Caitlyn's wrists, and she then started to struggle with the handcuffs, which were already twisting and bending into scrap. After a few moments of her straining with her full strength, the cuffs snapped, and Caitlyn had free hands.

"Hello, Claire," Allison could be heard saying from outside of the trailer.

"Yasmeen," Claire spat back. Now there were two vampires outside, and time was running out.

Caitlyn grabbed the platinum knife and slashed through her father's zip ties, but before they could make any further moves, the lock on the back door of the trailer could be heard being unlatched. The vampires were coming in, so Caitlyn stashed the knife in her pocket, and sat back down, pretending to still be bound.

The door opened, and both Allison and Claire stood in the entryway, and Claire had a bewildered look on her face. Allison ushered Claire into the trailer, guiding her right in front of the prisoners. "Pick one, and take them. Take from them, and let go of your mortal life. Let go of the chains that hold you down and be one of us, Claire."

Claire looked dumbfounded, as if trying to figure out what to do, but after a moment of silence and stillness, she grabbed Poppy and plunged her fangs into Poppy's neck. Poppy struggled for a moment, but the euphoria of Claire's kiss overwhelmed her in seconds. Claire didn't stop drinking from Poppy until she was dry, and when she finished, she dropped the body as if it were just an empty soda can. Caitlyn screamed in horror, but Claire didn't seem to hear her.

"Balthazar, Hades, and Persephone are all in a bunker under the hotel," Claire said, almost as if hypnotized. "If you hurry, you can still catch them."

"No need," said Allison. "We have a plan in place already. Come with me."

With that, Allison and Claire turned and left the trailer together, shutting the door behind them. Caitlyn, tears of heartbreak streaming down her face, clambered to her feet, slashing the zip ties and releasing the handcuffs that bound her ankles, and then freeing her father. She tried not to think about Poppy Armitage, because there was nothing that could be done for her now. She knew very little about the woman, beyond being tormented by the vampires for a long time, and being Claire's childhood friend, but now her suffering was over.

There would be far worse suffering if the Groves did not immediately leave the area.

Caitlyn closed the platinum knife, sliding it back into her pocket, gently patting the pocket and then turning to her father. "Can you walk?"

Ken nodded. "Yeah. The vamp didn't do anything to me but knock me out for a bit."

Caitlyn shot him an odd look. "Vamp? That's what we're calling them now?"

"Well, what would you call them?"

"A problem," Caitlyn spat. "Come on, we gotta get out of here."

"Wait," Ken said. "Did you feel that?"

"Feel wha…"

The world went white.

EPILOGUE

Silence had descended over what was once a noisy, busy city. Where once there had been bustling casinos, restaurants, and hotels, there was little more than smoking ruin. Where once busy streets were lined with thousands of people, there was only silence and smoldering ash. Las Vegas was utterly destroyed, and for the fortunate few who survived the blast, they had no idea why.

Underneath a pile of rubble and smoking debris, Caitlyn Grove had shielded her father from the worst effects of the blast, with only burns and minor injuries for her trouble. The climb out of the pile of debris was dangerous, but she protected her father all the way, and finally, they emerged to find a nightmare hellscape awaiting them. Dumbfounded, they looked around, only to find the city that they had seen only minutes before was no more. Only fire, ash, and smoke remained of Sin City.

"What in the fuck…?" Caitlyn whispered.

At that moment, in Washington, D.C., two figures stood in a darkened room, watching a bank of monitors. One, a smallish man with terrible hair and a repugnant face, had a look of utter disbelief on his face. The other, a tall, slim, pale woman, wore a broad smile, the sort that you'd find on a predator about to take down its meal.

"What have we done?" asked the man.

"Exactly what was intended," said the woman

As the sun was beginning to rise over the ruins of Las Vegas, a man came to a stop at a certain part of the ruined city. He looked down, crinkled his nose, and clucked his tongue. "This will never do. You aren't doing what you're meant to do if you're dead."

The man held his hands out before him and spoke in a loud voice. "Poppy, come forth!"

Deep within the rubble, someone opened their eyes, and began to scream.

OTHER BOOKS BY

BRITNEY EVERLONG

ALLISON'S GAME

HUNGER

TREE OF DEATH

JERICHO ROAD

BIRD OF PARADISE

BLOOD ROSES

ALL-AMERICAN DEAD GIRL

MAKE AMERICA DEAD AGAIN!

ALL CREEPING THINGS

RES OBSCURA